ENTER THE NEBULA

Start Publishing PD LLC
Copyright © 2024 by Start Publishing PD LLC

Start Publishing PD is a registered trademark of Start Publishing PD LLC
Manufactured in the United States of America

Cover art: Shutterstock/Taisiya Kozorez

Cover design: Jennifer Do

10 9 8 7 6 5 4 3 2 1

ISBN 979-8-8809-0431-0

ENTER THE NEBULA

by Carl Jacobi

The greatest cracksman in the Galaxy–The Nebula ... mocked by a gay voice that called herself Andromeda, who led him into danger–and into the hands of his enemy!

Phil Hanley came out of the managing editor's office and strode savagely to his desk in the paper littered city room. It was one P.M., between editions, and the reporters and copy-desk men of the *Martian Globe* were taking things easy for the moment. Hanley slumped into his chair, kicked his feet up on his auto-typewriter, and mouthed an oath. "He can't do it," he growled. "Who the hell does he think I am anyway? I'll quit, that's what I'll do."

"Not again," taunted McFee, a rewrite man.

"Yes, again," snarled Hanley. "And this time I mean it. Do you know what that lopsided jackass wants me to do? Get a personal interview with the Nebula. For all *I* know, the Nebula might be a four dimensional robot."

McFee lit a cigarette and leaned against the desk. "Did the old man really hand you that for an assignment?"

Hanley nodded, his anger passing now into glumness. "It's a compliment, I suppose," he said, "for anyone to think I might have even a chance." His eyes turned from the room and stared unseeing through the window into the metropolitan area of Crater City.

"The Nebula," he said slowly. "Every dick and I.P. man in the System has been tearing his hair, trying to get a lead on who or what he is. The Nebula! The greatest cracksman of all time!"

McFee exhaled a lungful of smoke. "He's quite a guy, isn't he?"

Deliberately Hanley dropped his feet to the floor and sat erect. "Listen," he said, "he's the Robin Hood of the day, if you can possibly remember your ancient history. Two years ago he swiped the electrolic jewels from the atomic motors of the *Fortuna*, the gambling space ship, broke them into two hundred parts and gave them to the Society for Orphaned Children. A year ago he entered the inner rooms of the Venus Gallery and made off with the *Cosmic Lady*, the greatest painting of the age.

"The man's a wizard. No vault door, no lock mechanism keeps him out. He walks in, takes what he wants, and leaves before the I.P. men know what's happened. All they find is that little pastel-blue card with the cluster of white

5

dots in the shape of the Constellation Orion. That's what gave him the name of the Nebula, you see."

McFee nodded. "I know," he said, "but who is he? And what's his permanent address?"

For a moment Hanley said nothing. He reached in his pocket, drew out a bulldog pipe and a worn tobacco pouch. A glitter was slowly entering his eyes. "You know," he said, "I have half a mind to try and find out at that."

*

The mercury clock over the white mantel chimed the hour of eight A.M., and Jimmy Starr sat up in bed yawning. As the last note faded into silence, the door of the room opened, and a white-haired man entered, carrying a tray.

"Good morning, Mr. Starr."

"Good morning, Peters," Jimmy said. "Did you bring the paper?"

The servant nodded, propped a morning edition against Jimmy's upraised knees and placed the breakfast tray on the side of the bed. "Will you have orange juice or Martian melon today?" he asked.

"Orange juice, I believe," replied Jimmy absently, and then coughed to hide the sudden tenseness that had entered his voice. He waited impatiently while the aged servant opened the window blinds and busied himself about the room.

When at last the man had gone, Jimmy sat bolt upright and stared at the screaming type.

NEBULA ON THE LOOSE AGAIN
GENTLEMAN BURGLAR PROVES
TO BE COMMON CRIMINAL

The running story was bitter in its denunciation. Where before those same columns had accepted each new exploit of the Nebula as a prank upon the police and an irritation to the wealthy, they now demanded legal action. For this time the Nebula had committed murder!

The Crater City Museum had been robbed during the night. Three priceless Thro-Pahl figurines had been stolen. An aged night watchman had been brutally beaten to death.

"The guilt is undeniable," the paper continued. "Drunk with power, this sadist had the effrontery to leave behind one of his mocking cards. What are the police going to do about it?"

Jimmy Starr leaned back and let a soft whistle escape from his lips. The newspaper story was all wrong. For Jimmy Starr had spent the entire night in his apartment. And Jimmy Starr was the Nebula!

He didn't know quite how long he had been playing this dual role. Years now, ever since his father, Randall Starr, president of the Triplanetary Freight Lines had been murdered and had left his enormous fortune to his son.

Randall Starr had come up from poverty with his only heritage, a brilliant mind and skillful hands. He had dabbled in a little of everything before he had become associated with the Venus-Mars-Earth shipping business. But all during his years of executive activity, he had always found time for two things: his hobby, the manufacture and study of theft-proof materials and devices; and the deciphering of the ancient *Lost Chronicles* of Mars.

It was this last that had resulted in his untimely end. Jimmy Starr had known for a long time that his father was on the verge of a great discovery, but what that discovery was he had had no inkling.

"Wait 'til I've finished," Randall Starr would always say when questioned. "Some day I'll have an announcement to make that will startle all Mars."

And then one night Jimmy Starr had been wakened by a terrific crash downstairs in the lower-floor study. He had rushed to the room to find his father stretched out on the floor, blood trickling from a gaping wound in his head. The window was open, showing the way of the assailant's escape. Randall Starr's filing cabinet had been thrown to the floor and battered open with some heavy instrument. Papers lay strewn about in wild disorder.

Jimmy knelt at his father's side, in time to hear the old man's last gasping words. "The ... Chronicles ... they took ... the five cyphers. You must get them back, Jimmy, before the last one is completed and the secret discovered.

You must, do you understand? The future of all life on this planet depends on it."

"Who...?" choked Jimmy. "Tell me who, and I'll...."

But the effort had been too great. The old man fell back, his warning unfinished.

Clues? Jimmy had employed the finest detectives on Mars in a vain attempt to track down the guilty one. He had followed trails himself, questioned all of his father's former friends and associates. The one and only shred of evidence he had led him no place. This was a polished *falpa* button which Randall Starr had torn from his assailant's tunic during the struggle—the type of button which members of the limited *superiors* class effected. The *superiors* were a throw-back to the feudalistic days of a by-gone age. Powerful overlords with inherited political and financial power, they still wielded a strong influence over an otherwise partially modernized society.

So this much Jimmy knew—his father had been murdered and the *Chronicles* cypher taken by a man who walked in the highest brackets of the System's social worlds.

*

In time Jimmy's grief passed, and he began to follow in his father's footsteps. Theoretically, he was acting head of Triplanetary. But with the shipping line operating smoothly with hundreds of efficient under-officials, there was little for him to do. After graduating from the Martian School of Technology, he toured the System in his own space-yacht. It was that trip that brought home to him the poverty and sordid conditions existent in the various worlds.

On Venus he had seen powerful land-owners growing fat and rich while native Kamalis and Sarakans toiled in the swamps. On Mars he had toured the luxurious plaisances and estates of the D.O.F.C—the Decedents of the First Colonists—and a hundred miles out in the desert had walked through the stinking narrow streets of the Thedras, the despised aboriginals of the West Plateaus.

Then and there Jimmy Starr had decided to add a twofold purpose to his life. He would do all in his power to aid the oppressed poor, and he would strain every effort to plague the lives of the *superiors* class. Some day, in some way, that effort would lead him, he felt sure, to his father's murderer and the stolen *Chronicles* cypher. The only item in question was the time element.

He spent six months in his father's private library, studying everything he could find on locks, time vaults, hermetic chambers and impenetrable walls. Six months more went into a thorough reading on the various subjects of criminology, micro-fingerprints, robot detectors.

He had begun quietly at first, a small art treasure taken from the collection of some greedy *superiors* millionaire. But gradually the daring of those thefts, the absolute lack of clues, with the exception of the tell-tale blue card, had attracted attention. In a year his fame had spread as far as Pluto. In six months more the Nebula was a byword in every tongue.

The police had sworn action, the press had chuckled, and the public had looked with open admiration on this benefactor of the downtrodden.

Now all that was over. The Nebula was a criminal. He was accused of murder.

Slowly Jimmy Starr got out of bed and began to dress. Funny, he had never thought of this contingency. Someone had seen an opportunity to profit by his name, and had utilized it with cold-blooded efficiency.

He lit a cheroot and stood there smoking. A bell tinkled behind him, announcing a call on the visiphone. He crossed to the panel, touched a stud. A voice came out of the speaker, but no image appeared on the vision screen.

"*Good morning, Nebula!*"

An electric shock swept through him. His cheroot slipped from his fingers.

"*Good morning, Nebula. Answer please.*"

Mechanically Jimmy's fingers found the transmitting button and clicked it over. But he stood out of range of the vision screen as he replied, "Who's speaking?"

The feminine voice, sweet and musical, laughed gaily. "I'm sorry I can't tell you that. You may call me Andromeda, if you will. Now listen closely, Jimmy

9

Starr. I know your secret. I know that you live a dual life, that you are that much sought after gentleman cracksman, the Nebula."

The voice laughed again, but there was no mockery in it. "You needn't be afraid, Jimmy, I'm not going to let the cat out of the bag. But I will, unless you agree to follow my orders. Is that clear?"

For a long moment Jimmy stood there in silence.

"Never mind," the voice continued, "I didn't expect you to admit it. But listen. The Nebula is no longer a champion of the poor. In the eyes of the press and the police, he has committed murder. I know that you are innocent of that charge. It is now eight-thirty. In exactly fifteen hours you will go to the central offices of the Crater City Trust Company at Ninth and Planet. You will enter in any way you see fit, open the vault and take from the compartment marked W-203 the three articles it contains. Do you understand? Compartment W-203."

There was a click and the visiphone was silent.

Frantically Jimmy twisted the control switch on and off. "Hello," he said, "hello!"

*

He turned slowly to face the looking glass on the opposite wall mirrored the sudden haggardness that had entered his features. In half an hour his entire world had crashed. His identity was known. He was wanted for a foul crime.

Yes, he had been hunted before, but now the police and the I.P. men would leave no stone unturned in their efforts to capture him. His pursuers would be relentless.

He paced to the window and looked down on the Martian city. To the east where the main sky ramp led to the city's space port lay the huge ditch that was the beginning of Canal Grand. Like a crayon smear on a piece of cardboard, it stretched off into the desert, bleak and desolate.

*

At fifteen minutes past eleven that night Jimmy Starr opened a panel in his room and took his place in a cylindrical shell, touched a control and settled back. Save for a slight jar and an audible hum, there was no sensation of movement. Moments later the tube-cage jarred again, the door slid open, and he climbed out on a small lighted kiosk in the center of a well of darkness. A narrow ramp led upward, and he made his way to the street level in a few quick strides.

He now stood on the intersection of Ninth and Planet.

Jimmy Starr sauntered across the street, studying each passerby out of the corner of his eyes. Before the entrance of the Crater City Trust Company he paused to light a cheroot. He stood there, smoking quietly while a turbaned Kagor from the North Desert Country shuffled by, dragging his cumbersome third leg after him.

Then he slipped open his tunic, exposing a small compact carry-case strapped about his middle. Opening it, he selected from its array of objects a slender metal tube, capped at one end. To this he quickly fastened a small ball of hardened carponium clay. He unscrewed a cap in the clay ball and inserted a small pellet.

With flying fingers, he shoved the tube hard against the door lock. That lock was not the best, but it was one of the most dependable theft-proof devices on the market.

Mentally he counted the seconds as each pulsation within the tube was transmitted to his hand. At the tenth he stiffened. There was a dull thud, a little puff of smoke, and a grating and jangling as of breaking glass.

Then he was inside, pacing down the center aisle of the main office. He had no need for a torch. The place was brilliantly lighted with overhead carboliers, and he knew that he was clearly visible from the street.

In rapid strides he reached the far end of the office, where an enormous vault door of *arelium* steel was imbedded in a frame of *kartite*. That frame was anchored in natural rock piers ninety feet below. The entire structure was as impregnable as human intellect could make it.

Jimmy Starr leaped over the low railing that separated the vault from the office proper. Again he opened the little carry-case and from a lower compartment took out a tightly rolled Martian papyrus.

He was working fast now, putting into action a plan that he had formed on his visit to this office earlier in the day. Then, while he had stood discussing the financial status of Triplanetary Shipping with one of the Trust Company officials, he had managed to slip out a tiny camera and, unobserved, take a quick photograph of the rear wall of the office.

Back in his own apartment it had been the work of a few moments to transfer the scene on the negative onto this elastic papyrus.

He stood up on the railing, fastened the two ends of the papyrus to the side wall; then, utilizing all his strength, stretched it across the full width of the office to the opposite wall.

Finished, he slipped behind the screen with a gay laugh. Let a passerby gaze in the street window now. He would see a deserted office with the unmolested vault in clear view. From the street no one could know that vault was an enlarged photograph on a screen, and that behind that screen crouched the most wanted cracksman on Mars—the Nebula!

He spent a moment surveying the massive vault. "Craig-Orlan, Series A. Model Four," he muttered appreciatively. "Mercury time lock, rondulated tumblers, protected with individual micacaps. This is going to be tough."

He took from the carry-case a pair of earphones, snapped them on and pressed their connection to the panel just below the main dial. Slowly he began to turn that dial, straining his ears for tell-tale clicks.

The silence of the office pressed down upon him. Far off sounded the hollow roar as the night Earth Express blasted down to its cradle.

For several minutes he continued. Then his brow furrowed in a frown. "Must have a shield of some kind behind it," he muttered. He opened the carry-case again, drew forth a tiny electrolic drill with a wedge-shaped bit. A low hum sounded as he switched the drill on and pressed it against the panel.

When an aperture of half an inch in depth had been bored, he removed the drill and placed in the opening another of his pellets. Ten seconds and the puff of blue smoke. Once more he slipped on the headphones.

This time a smile of satisfaction turned his lips. In the receivers he could hear distinctly each metallic click as the grooved tumblers fell into position.

He reached up now and shoved a huge *kapar* bar far over in its slot. On silent hinges the enormous vault door began to open.

But this was only the beginning. It was a full hour before he had penetrated the second and third inner doors of the vault, another half hour before he located in the vast array of files, Compartment W-203.

*

About to open it, he stood motionless in thought. What was he doing here? Why was he ransacking the vault of the Crater City Trust, one of the most respected and ethical financial institutions in the city? He wanted nothing of theirs. More than that, there was a murder charge on his head, and he was deliberately taking chances when all logic screamed at him to hide.

As in a dream he heard that musical voice that had come over the visiphone, "*Listen, Jimmy Starr, I know your secret....*" He inserted a false key in the file lock and opened it.

Nothing! The compartment was empty.

A wave of bitterness swept over him. He thrust the compartment shut savagely and turned to leave the vault. Half way he halted in mid-stride.

A sound had reached his ears from the opposite side of the papyrus screen, the sound of someone fumbling with the latch of the front entrance door.

Quickly Jimmy passed through the three doors of the vault. He paused before the combination to slide a small card under the dial. Pastel-blue in color, that card bore the design of the constellation Orion.

Then he reached up, whipped down the papyrus screen and crouched back of the railing. The man at the front entrance had discovered the broken lock; the door crashed open; excited footsteps pounded inward.

Bending low, Jimmy darted down the side aisle, keeping his head well below the top of the desks. Once he shot a look at the intruder. It was Hamilton Garth, president of Crater City Trust! A gray-haired man with a wiry build, an iron visage, and heavy-browed gimlet eyes. Before the yawning door of the vault Garth stopped short and uttered a cry of consternation. He spun on his heel and with rapid strides made for the door.

But not before Jimmy had reached it. He raced through the entrance just as Garth sighted him and gave a hoarse shout.

Jimmy raced down the street a hundred yards, then hurled himself into an alley. A police officer was running toward him, attracted by Garth's cries.

Even as Jimmy crouched there, new sounds added to the confusion. The alarm tocsin of the Crater City Trust shrilled up and up into the rarified air. Far down the street the answering siren of the I.P. depot rose in deafening crescendo. Jimmy could hear windows bang open in the buildings across the thoroughfare. The emergency street lamps flared on, turning the intersection into a stage of ghastly white.

The alley-way in which he crouched was a dead-end. Jimmy thrust aside the wave of helplessness that swept over him and steeled himself for action. The Nebula couldn't be caught. Not now with brutality dogging his footsteps.

With a swift movement he whipped off the tunic, threw it from him. Frantically he opened the carry-case and took from it a short collapsible rod, a folded rakish evening cap. He shoved the carry-case under his waist coat, hoping that the bulge would not be detected, set the cap on his head at a jaunty angle and jerked the rod out to its full four feet.

That rod was an explosive detonator for use on time doors when all other means of entrance failed. But it was a cane now. Swinging it, Jimmy darted out into the glare of the street, then began to pace leisurely forward straight in the direction of Crater City Trust.

When he reached the entrance, a small crowd had gathered, and Hamilton Garth was in their midst excitedly talking to an I.P. officer.

"Vault doors wide open!" he was shouting. "Second and third doors, too! It's the Nebula! I saw his card. Why the devil don't you do something?"

The I.P. man was taking notes in a little book. "Calm yourself, Mr. Garth," he said. "Whoever broke in here can't get away this time. The impenetration walls have automatically closed down. The entire area is cut off by a ring of steel."

"But it's the Nebula I tell you, you stupid fool!" cried Garth. "While you stand there like an idiot—" The eyes of the Trust Company president suddenly fastened on Jimmy, leaning comfortably on his rod-cane at the edge of the growing crowd. "Mr. Starr, I'm certainly glad to see you. Help me. Tell me what I should do...."

Nodding quietly, Jimmy stepped forward. To the I.P. he said casually, "J. C. Starr, president of Triplanetary Shipping. How much has been stolen, officer?"

Another I.P. man emerged from the Trust office. "Only one compartment opened, sir. W-203."

Hamilton Garth looked bewildered. "That's odd," he said. "The W series of files are all unused. There's nothing in any of them."

Jimmy laughed. "Mr. Garth, you can consider yourself a lucky man. The Nebula seems to have muffed things this time. Good night."

He turned and sauntered off down the street.

*

It was the following morning, and for an hour Jimmy Starr had sat by the visiphone in his room, waiting for a call. A tray of half-smoked cheroots lay on the table beside the instrument.

The bell sounded. Jimmy touched the stud.

"*Good morning, Nebula. We failed last night, didn't we?*"

He leaned back in his chair and smiled. Though that haunting musical voice stirred him deeply, he had full control of himself now. For an hour he had been preparing mentally what he would say.

"Young woman," he said, "or Andromeda, as you choose to call yourself, I haven't the slightest idea of what you're talking about. Yesterday you made a connection with my instrument and hung up without revealing your image. My name is James C. Starr, and if you wish to converse with me, I suggest you show yourself. Otherwise...."

"Wait!" The gayness left the unseen girl's voice. "Wait, don't touch that stud. We failed last night, Jimmy Starr. But we can't fail again tonight. Everything is at stake. Do you understand, everything. The very future of life here on Mars. Jimmy, what do you know about the canals?"

15

"The canals?" He forgot his protestations to consider thoughtfully. "Why nothing much. They're to be opened and filled with water in a year. Everyone knows that. So far the locks have been giving the engineers a little trouble, but...."

"Not a little trouble, Jimmy. A whole lot of trouble. At the present time specifications call for a hundred and twelve locks and sub power stations down the length of Canal Grand alone. And there are seven hundred and eight subsidiary canals branching into the main stem. Add to those figures the number of lesser canals branching into the subsidiary canals, the necessary freight and passenger depots, and you can see what a tremendous engineering project it will be."

"It can be done," Jimmy said confidently.

"It can, yes, if the engineers locate a new deposit of *pxar*, the part organic, part inorganic material that alone will withstand the terrible refraction-rot of the red desert country."

Jimmy didn't know what she was driving at, but what she said was true. Refraction-rot, the multiple infra-red light radiations from the scarlet sands of the desert played hob with all kinds of construction work. *Pxar* alone had the resiliency and the hardness to withstand the terrible disintegration processes of the shifting sands. And there was very little *pxar* left.

The voice continued:

"Jimmy, I can't tell you everything yet. But I can tell you this. By joining forces with me, you will be working toward the recovery of your father's lost secret and the identification of the man who murdered him.

"Tonight at midnight you will enter the offices of Phobos Enterprises and take from their vault the paper-wrapped box on the third shelf. Good luck, Nebula."

*

Phil Hanley, reporter of the *Globe*, let himself into his apartment, strode straight to the liquor cabinet and took a stiff drink. Then he sat down before a table and spread an array of objects before him.

They were a curious collection: A polished *falpa* button of the type affected by members of the *superiors* class; two panelled cards, each with the design of the Constellation Orion, two rather blurred photographs of finger prints, and a notebook.

These findings were the results of Hanley's activities during the night. Still obsessed with his plan to get a signed interview with the Nebula, he had reasoned, logically enough, that the only way to do so was to learn first the cracksman's identity.

The button first. It was elliptical in shape and bore that curious triangular emblem so hated by the poorer classes. Hanley had found it on the office floor of the Crater City Trust Company. He realized, however, that any number of *superiors* might have business with that establishment and that the button's presence there meant nothing.

In rotation he examined the two panelled cards and the fingerprint photographs. He brought a powerful atolight down and studied them with the aid of a *proberglass*.

At the end of five minutes a low whistle of amazement came to his lips. He pushed glass and light away and brought forward the discovery he had deliberately reserved for the last. The notebook.

There was no reason to believe it the property of the Nebula. The Nebula didn't go around dropping private journals for inquisitive reporters to find. Hanley had discovered it half hidden in the gutter before the entrance of the Crater City Museum where the night watchman had been murdered.

The notebook contained but a single page of writing. In heavy penmanship the words read:

The figurines are pure pxar. The breakdown analysis will prove that, I am sure. But whether the figurines will serve their intended purpose is a question that can be answered only by experiment. If my decipherment of the Chronicles is correct, I must have thousands of them, and to obtain them it will be necessary to locate the Tombs. Does the marking Ka Ce 54 W bear any significance?

ENTER THE NEBULA

Phil Hanley read those words twice, then leaned back, frowning. Presently he roused himself, strode to a wall cabinet and took down a book labeled, *Ancient Mars—the Webley Theories of the Early Life*.

He carried the book back to the table, but before he could open it, steps sounded along the outer corridor leading to his door. A moment later the door banged open, and a figure crossed the threshold.

Hanley had but a split instant to utter a gasp of astonished recognition. Then he saw the heat gun leveled directly at him, and with a twisting leap, he lunged for the connecting door of the adjoining room.

*

Jimmy Starr was panting when he reached his room. The clock on the mantel showed five A.M., and since midnight he had been living with double interest his role as a fugitive.

Without realizing why, he had obeyed to the letter the instructions of the voice on the visiphone. That single suggestion that his efforts might lead him to the murderer of his father had spurred him on. He had entered Phobos Enterprises, taken the package described. But getting away this time had been a terrible ordeal.

The I.P. men were on the alert. All Crater City patrols were in readiness. The impenetration walls were down everywhere, checkerboarding the metropolis into five hundred separate and distinct guarded areas.

Three times he had missed capture by a scant margin. He had crawled sixty feet through an exhaust *zordite* tube when any second the motors leading to it might have seared his body to a crisp with their discharges. With an I.P. man close on his heels, he had swung over a dizzy canyon of space and catwalked across a sustaining bar from one building to another. And it seemed now he could still hear that cry that rose up to him on the building roof from the street below:

"*Death to the Nebula!*"

On the table the package for which he had risked so much lay open. Jimmy scowled down upon its contents: three Thro-Pahl figurines, gray in color, eighteen inches in height, each the likeness of an armor-clad Martian of the first dynasty. To an art collector they were undoubtedly wondrous artifacts, but to Jimmy they meant nothing.

The visiphone bell sounded. Heart pounding, Jimmy touched the stud and heard again that voice.

"*Good morning, Nebula. We made it this time. I'm so glad.*"

He stared into the blank screen silently. What did she look like, the owner of that haunting voice? Was she dark or fair? Was she...? "Who are you?" he said huskily.

"There isn't time for that now, Jimmy. Tell me, have you examined the figurines?"

He had the vision plate turned on, and he nodded in reply.

"Look at them again. Look at their composition. It's not the carving I'm—we're—interested in. It's their structure. Don't you see, Jimmy? It's *pxar*."

He didn't see, and he waited for her to continue.

"*Pxar*—the same material that the engineers need for their construction work for the canal locks, the only material that will withstand the radiations of the Red Desert sands.

"Those figurines are old, Jimmy. They were carved during the days of the First Dynasty when the original canal locks were built. Today there's practically none left. Yet without *pxar* the canal project is doomed to failure.

"Now pick up one of the figurines and examine its base. Do you see that tiny three-cornered prong that projects from it? Like a root, a stunted root reaching out for nourishment."

*

The girl's voice became breathless. "Jimmy, that was your father's secret. He spent the last days of his life deciphering the *Lost Chronicles*, and for years it has been my work too. You see, chemical analysis has proved that under certain conditions *pxar* will grow and reproduce its own kind. The early Martians knew this, and they also knew that the time would come when there would be no more of it available. So they designed those figurines to be superimposed on the bodies of living Martians. The root-claw would then reach down, embed itself in the flesh and suck out the vital life."

"I—I don't understand," Jimmy said slowly.

"Let me put it this way. If the base of one of those figurines is fastened to the body of a Martian, the root will adhere to that body, and the figurine will become a living parasite, growing and developing in size, until amoeba-like, it will divide into two.

"Jimmy, there's a monstrous plot brewing here on Mars. Your father discovered that secret and realized it was so deadly he meant to lock it away forever in the files of the Interplanetary Council. But before he could do that, he was murdered and the incomplete cyphers stolen. Those cyphers have now been worked out. Someone has made plans to sell an enormous quantity of *pxar* to the development company that's building the canal locks. They're going to create that *pxar* by feeding those figurines and thousands like them off the bodies of unsuspecting Martians."

"But how?" Jimmy interjected.

"I don't know how. Not yet, though I've been piecing the threads of this puzzle together for weeks now. It wasn't until five days ago that I was able to decipher completely the code of the *Chronicles*. I did know that your father was working on the cypher, too, because he and I frequented the same libraries, but it was only by accident that I discovered that that cypher was the reason behind his murder.

"Once started, the *pxar* plot will be a plague, a Martian black death. Once started, those figurines will multiply and grow. And here's the damnable part of it, Jimmy. After a certain number of the figurines have been given life, they will also acquire self mobility. Do you understand? It means that they will spread, advance from the body of one Martian to another of their own accord. That's the black revelation of the *Chronicles—the fact that this plague happened on this planet once before, was responsible for the complete extinction of the first dynasty Martians.*"

He turned the gray figurine over and over in his hands. There was a glitter in his eyes now, a glitter of excitement. Things were falling into place in his brain like pieces of a puzzle.

"Examine those images," the girl's voice suddenly ordered. "Do you see any mark on them at all?"

One by one he studied every inch of their surfaces. Abruptly his eyes caught a tiny series of even scratches along the thigh of one of the figurines.

"Ka Ce 54 W," he read slowly.

For a moment silence answered him. Then the voice uttered a low gasp. "It's the first section of the third cypher," she said. "It means ... wait a minute ... it means that the Tombs are in the Dur-Par section of the desert. Jimmy, we've got to go there."

"The Tombs?" he repeated.

"Yes, according to the *Chronicles*, a secret store of thousands of those parasitical figurines is hidden somewhere out in the Red Desert. The first dynasty Martians, you see, prepared for the emergency which they knew was inevitable, the disappearance of *pxar* from this planet. That was before they knew of the images' plague properties.

"We've got a race on our hands, Jimmy. Even now the man who first stole the figurines may be heading directly for the Tombs."

Jimmy Starr took out a cheroot, lit it mechanically. Then he voiced a single question. "You must have a personal interest in this matter. What is it?"

She had the answer for that too. "My brother," she said, "is one of the technical officials for the canal-locks project. A murder charge was framed on him, and he was given the alternative of being 'exposed' to the I.P. men or agreeing to accept all the *pxar* an unidentified source could supply with no questions asked. He has agreed.

"I ... I love my brother, but this has gone beyond personalities now. This is plague, wholesale murder; all Mars is at stake."

Jimmy Starr made an instant decision. "Where will I meet you?" he said.

She considered. Then, "You'll find instructions at the Canal Grand entrance. Good luck, Jimmy."

*

ENTER THE NEBULA

Half an hour later Jimmy climbed out of a tube-cage and emerged onto a deserted square at the outskirts of Crater City. Before him, dim in the overhead light, a sign read:

THE CANALS
POSITIVELY NO TRESPASSING
ENTER AT YOUR OWN RISK

Before the sign stood a small kiosk with dusty bulletins tacked upon it. Jimmy waited impatiently, pacing to and fro. Then his eye caught sight of a small envelope protruding from a crevice on the kiosk wall. It bore no name or address, but upon its surface was the design of the Constellation Orion.

Inside, a scrap of paper bore the written words: "*Canal Grand—south. Way Station X. I'll meet you there.*"

He pursed his lips. What kind of a game was this? Unseen speakers on the visiphone. Mysterious messages directing him into the unknown. It smacked of a twentieth century thriller.

All his inherent sense of danger warned him to turn back. In answer, that haunting voice rang again in his ears: "*Good luck, Jimmy.*"

He turned to the stair well and began to descend. Darkness was here, and he could feel the thick red dust under his shoes as he went down. Fifty-seven ... fifty-eight ... first ... second ... third level. Not until he reached the bottom and stood before the massive door leading into the canal did he switch on his electric torch. Then he stared.

The door yawned open. Twenty feet beyond, drawn up at the near wall of the great ditch, was a tracto-car. And before that car there were three men preparing to board.

Jimmy stared as he recognized the foremost of the three. Hamilton Garth! The Trust Company official stood there calmly in the glare of the torch, waiting for him to approach.

"What the devil are you doing here?" Garth demanded.

It was a tight question, but fortunately Garth was so absorbed in his own plans and movements that he did not wait for an answer. "Sloan and

Barker," he said shortly, waving his hand toward his two companions. "I.P. men. We're trailing the Nebula."

"But I thought nothing was stolen from your office," Jimmy said slowly. "You said...."

Garth scowled. "Money, tangibles, no. But prestige, tremendously. Do you realize, sir, what it will mean when the public learns that a cheap cracksman can walk into my vault as if it had a revolving door? I've offered fifty thousand *plantoles* for the arrest of the Nebula, and I'm going to set an example by being the first to start on his trail."

"I see." Jimmy studied him in thoughtful silence. "And his trail starts here?"

"In the canal, yes. We received an unsigned tip half an hour ago that the Nebula was heading south down Canal Grand. You're coming with us, of course."

As the tracto-car rocketed dizzily down the huge ditch, Jimmy hunkered down in the tonneau seat and let his thoughts run wild. This tip Garth had spoken of.... Could it be that she...?

He forced his eyes toward the way ahead, deliberately guiding his mind into other channels. It wasn't the first time he had been in the canals, but it was the first time he had penetrated this far. The powerful triple-beam atolight cut a swath of radiance ahead like a chalkmark on a blackboard. Revealed in its glare were the mountainous-high walls of red stone on either side, the red floor between, hard packed, smooth as a pavement. Dimly in the reflected glow he could see the serrated lines high up near the top of the near wall, the marks of the ancient water levels, and at intervals he could see the crumbling ruins of a counting depot.

What glory, what pomp and circumstance this mighty ditch had seen. Gilded canopied barges of the first and second dynasty kings, military floats, ore and shipping rafts, all drifting in an endless procession across the arid wastes of the Red Desert. Army transports loaded with armored troops advancing and retreating, converging through the labyrinthian network of subsidiary canals to battle the capital itself.

ENTER THE NEBULA

And today the wonders of the past were on the verge of being repeated. Engineers were struggling frantically to overcome the one problem that so far had baffled them—the finding of a supply of *pxar* sufficient to rebuild the locks.

Ahead a lone Kiloto swooped out of the darkness into the span of light, whirled frantically and missed the onrushing car by inches.

Presently a low rubble of masonry loomed before them. Hamilton Garth tapped the I.P. man driver on the shoulder. "Way station," he said. "Pull in there. We'll look for clues."

It was a forlorn spot. A few *pxar* columns stood sentinel-like at the entrance. A roofless plaisance stretched beyond. Here and there were the remnants of crude hydro-dovolic mechanism chambers. Hamilton Garth made a thorough examination of the place with his torch. The search was fruitless, of course, and he stood up with a scowl.

"I suggest we split up and look around outside," he said. "Sloan, you take the east side; Barker, take the right, and I'll go straight down the canals for a ways. Mr. Starr, you'd better stay here, if you don't mind."

It suited Jimmy. This was the place where he was scheduled to meet Andromeda, and the sooner he could be alone, the better. Even now he was tingling with excitement at the thought of unveiling the owner of that hidden voice.

*

The two I.P. men and Garth shuffled off into the sand. Silence and the loneliness of the Martian night closed in on Jimmy. He crossed to a block of stone and slumped down on it wearily. From far off somewhere the banshee scream of a prowler shattered the stillness. It died away, came again, and then merged eerily into the wail of an Enzo-cat, the two-headed carrion-eater of the desert. And then suddenly a voice behind him said, "Don't look now, Jimmy, but a friend of yours is here."

He wheeled and brought up the electric torch as simultaneously a hand grasped his.

"Not here, Jimmy. No light, please. Come, there's not a moment to lose."

A slender figure was partly visible in the gloom. A faint scent of Martian *trofero* touched his nostrils.

Before he could protest further he found himself guided out of the Way Station and out into the sand. Presently a small two-seater tracto-car rose up before them. There was no sign of Garth or the two I.P. men. The girl leaped in, touched a stud, and the car trembled with life. Two seconds later they were boring into the darkness.

"Can I look now?" Jimmy demanded.

She laughed. "If you like."

He switched on the torch. A young dark-haired girl with clear brown eyes and lovely features smiled back at him. She was beautiful.

He settled deeper in the seat. "Garth and the two I.P. men. Why didn't they come back?"

She didn't reply to that. Savagely with a sudden frantic twist of the wheel she maneuvered the tracto-car on a tangent toward the east bank of the canal. Even as she did, a man-high ribbon of white irridescence shot toward them. It was a spear-headed ellipse of blinding light with a whipping comet-like tail.

"Refraction-protract," she cried. Under her skillful guidance the car turned left, then right, to miss the oncoming beam by inches. The girl uttered a sigh of relief. "That was too close for comfort," she said. "Those refraction-protracts are disintegrating light rays stored up by the Red Desert sands and released by sudden changes in temperature. We'll have to watch ourselves."

They drove on in silence. Questions were surging through Jimmy's brain, but he said nothing, waiting for the girl to explain.

"Would it surprise you very much if I told you the man behind all this is Hamilton Garth?"

He went slowly rigid. "Garth? But he—"

"Told you he was trailing the Nebula. That was a neat way to divert suspicion from himself. You see, Garth, although a member of the *superiors* class, has been having financial trouble with both of his companies lately, Crater City Trust, and Phobos Enterprises. Some of his investments went wrong; in particular, an expedition he financed to Pluto was never heard from again. He needed funds desperately and *pxar* was his answer.

"How he learned that your father's work in deciphering the *Chronicles* was connected with this strange material, we probably shall never know. The important thing is he did find out and immediately took steps to acquire them. But even after he had them it was necessary to complete the cypher before he could learn the secret. Garth must have found a passage in some work other than the *Chronicles* that led him to suspect vaguely the nature of the final revelation."

Jimmy nodded slowly. "I see," he said. "And after Garth has located the supply of figurines, he intends to launch them on their parasitical work and sell the supply of *pxar* he thus accumulates to the engineers. But neither the Martians nor the engineers would consent to such a diabolical plan."

The girl smiled grimly and touched a stud on the dash, increasing the speed of the car. "Garth took care of that, too," she explained. "He planned to advertise all over Mars a sanitarium devoted to the cure of every conceivable kind of ill. It was to be located in the mountains beyond the Red Desert Country. Once a patient was admitted, his doom was sealed.

"It was Garth, of course, who broke into the Crater City Museum, stole the three Thro-Pahl figurines and killed the night-watchman. Previously he had designed a fake Nebula signature card, and he left this behind at the scene of the crime. He's a member of the *superiors* class, you must remember, and his hatred for the man who was making a mockery of that class was intense."

*

Dawn came up slowly, a reddish haze at first, then a brilliant glare that turned the canal into a glittering avenue of crimson reflections. They roared east along a canal that steadily grew narrower.

Presently, far ahead, a depression became visible in the side wall. Up this depression a nature-formed ramp led to the upper level.

"This is the end of the line," the girl said. She gave a short laugh. "Do you realize, Mr. Starr, you haven't even asked me my name?"

He colored, stammered something.

"It's Linda," she said, "Linda Hall. Come. Up this way."

The climb was hard, grueling work, and when at length they reached the summit, man and girl were panting from the exertion. But here Jimmy looked upon a scene of utter desolation. As far as the eye could reach stretched a vast plain. No cairn, no monolithic pile of rocks broke the bleak monotony.

Linda, however, moved forward with a quick step. She had a small metal box with needle dials in her hand now, and she consulted it at intervals. For a quarter of a mile they plodded across the flat. Then Jimmy saw that the needles on the dials were fluttering wildly.

"Stand here," she told him.

She moved off on a tangent, walking carefully, studying the ground. He watched her figure grow smaller and smaller. Abruptly she halted and waved to him frantically. He hurried to her side.

She stood at the brink of a deep cleft in the plain floor. Rectangular in shape, it seemed to bore down and down into measureless depths. Jimmy felt his heart skip a beat. A flight of ladder-like stairs descended into the well, and lying prone at the top of those stairs was a man.

A deep searing burn ran from his temple down the left side of his face, about which blood had caked and hardened. Jimmy knelt and fumbled for a pulse. A faint flutter touched his fingers. He whipped a flask from his pocket and brought it to the man's lips.

He moaned, opened his eyes weakly and rose up on one elbow.

"Who are you?" Jimmy demanded.

At first his words were unintelligible. Then the haze which clouded his eyes cleared somewhat.

"Name's Hanley," he said weakly. "Phil Hanley. Represent the *Martian Globe*. Hamilton Garth's down there. We've got to stop him."

Hanley struggled with short jerky sentences. "Garth blasted me with a heat gun. Tried to do it once before in my own apartment, but I managed to get away from him. This time he thought he'd done for me. He's after the figurines. *By the blazing eternal! Are you the Nebula?*"

ENTER THE NEBULA

*

Six hundred and thirty-nine steps led to the bottom of the shaft. In places the rock had crumbled so badly the greatest care had to be taken, or a misstep would have meant plunging into the abyss. Curiously, no sand seemed to have drifted here; the air was dry and clear.

Hanley, still unsteady from the burn he had received, examined the hieroglyphics on the stone walls with puzzled eyes.

"This place must have been discovered before," he said. "It isn't possible that this shaft could have remained here all these years without someone stumbling upon it."

Linda nodded. "It's presence has been known, of course," she replied. "It leads to an underground cavern that stretches for miles under the surface. It's the burial place of the first dynasty Martians. But there are many such places below the Red Desert country. Always it has been thought they contained nothing of value."

They reached the bottom level and stood staring out before them. Where the floor of the desert above had been red in color, the surface here was ochre, a dull uncertain floor that gave off a radiance of its own and illuminated the underground cavern with a faint unreal glow. The grotto stretched in three directions as far as the light permitted them to see. At intervals of every twenty feet or so, large rectangular blocks, ten to fifteen feet high and twelve feet long, dotted the expanse. In a way the place looked like a vast apiary.

"Each one is a grave," Linda said quietly. "The block, of course, is only a marker. The crypt is lower down."

Jimmy scowled. "And one of those crypts contains the figurines, eh? Like looking for a needle in a haystack."

She gripped his arm. "We've got to find the right one before Garth. We've got to, do you understand! He's somewhere down here now, with those two hirelings of his. When—if—we do find it, this will destroy them." She pressed a short tube in Jimmy's hands.

Like three sleep-walkers, they paced slowly out among the stone blocks. And now Jimmy realized the proportions of the task they had set themselves to do. Each of the blocks was equipped with a vault-like door of massive weight and size, surrounded by a panel of those strange hieroglyphics, and with an intricate series of bizarre lock dials on its surface. The blocks looked exactly the same.

Above them in the dimness of the ceiling a heavy whirring sounded, and at intervals a curious bird-like creature with pointed wings and a weazened human face swooped down to be momentarily visible in the half light.

"*Sarkonivals*," Linda said shortly. "The early Martians were superstitious of them and transported them here to guard the burial grounds. They must feed on a variety of moss that grows down here."

They moved on. The rows of burial blocks seemed endless. Jimmy came to a halt.

"We're getting no place fast," he said. "Have you no clue at all as to which block it might be?"

Linda shook her head. Hanley was staring up above him, apparently fascinated by the strange flying creatures.

"You know," he said slowly, "I read about those *sarkonivals* once. They always fly in groups of an even twenty, save when some atmospheric disturbance causes them to alter their formation."

He pointed upward. "They *are* all in groups of twenty except over that block over there. Above that they seem to be in confusion."

Jimmy followed his gaze and frowned thoughtfully. He paced forward to the block in question, stood there watching the movements of the *sarkonivals*.

Suddenly he turned to Linda. "Look. See how their flying formation is always the same? They're twenty of them up there all right, and they start to circle the block in a compact mass. But as soon as they strike a point directly above it, they separate. First five, then three, then two, six, one, and three. Always the same order. Do you suppose that might be the combination? A magnetic disturbance issuing from the block in such a way as to prevent the usual twenty-formation and break it up in that fashion?"

"Jimmy!" Her eyes lighted. "I think you've got it!"

He seized the ancient combination wheel, put his strength to it. Slowly, a fraction of an inch at a time, it began to turn. Jimmy hesitated.

"I can't read these numerals, if they are numerals," he said. "I don't know where to start."

Linda studied the markings. "I think that's the symbol for absolute zero," she said. "Try it anyway."

He began to turn the wheel again, counting off the numbers as he watched the irregular formation of *sarkonivals* above him. "Five, three, two, six, one, three."

Twice he tried with no result. The third time there was a dull whirring somewhere in the bowels of the block, and the door slowly swung open. Within, a short passageway ended at another door, equipped with another series of dials.

Here Jimmy nodded in satisfaction. "I should be able to crack this."

He opened his carry-case, took out the headphones and slipped them on. Linda and Hanley pressed close, watching him.

"Hurry," the girl said. "I don't like it here."

A voice behind answered her.

"No need to hurry, Mr. Starr, alias the Nebula. Just take your time, but be sure you open it."

*

They wheeled. Three figures blocked the passage. In the lead, leaning comfortably against the side wall, stood Hamilton Garth, a heat gun leveled before him. Behind him were the two pseudo-I.P. men.

"Very nice of you to save us the trouble of locating the figurine cache," Garth said smoothly. "Now all you have to do is open that inner door and then help us carry a load of the images back to our tracto-car. You have nothing to worry about. If you obey orders, no harm will come to you. If you don't, well, don't forget I have a nice ace-in-the-hole. I have only to tell the world that James C. Starr, president of Triplanetary Shipping is the much-wanted cracksman, the Nebula."

Jimmy, Linda, and Hanley looked at each other.

"Come," said Garth. "This place oppresses me as much as it does you. Get to work."

Silently Jimmy adjusted the headphones again and began to move the dials. Five minutes passed. Then he stood back, grasped the handle and pulled the door open.

The interior was black, but a click of the torch revealed row upon row of Thro-Pahl images. There were hundreds here, and there must be hundreds more in the lower crypt.

And then Jimmy remembered the metal tube Linda had given him when they first entered this underground chamber. He drew forth the tube and with a quick motion threw it before him.

Nothing! The crypt remained steeped in silence.

"What was that you threw?" demanded Garth. "Answer, damn you!"

Jimmy shrugged. "It was a tube of setro-frenalot—NSK 54," he said. "I think you know what that means, Mr. Garth. The double detonation explosive. If it doesn't explode upon the first impact, the slightest jar, the slightest whisper of sound will discharge it."

Garth's face went black with rage. "You damned double-crossing—!"

He tossed his heat gun to one of the two pseudo-I.P. men and plunged into the vault. Halfway the significance of Jimmy's words came home to him. Gingerly, a step at a time, he began to work his way toward the metal tube that lay in the light of his electric torch.

Now he stood directly above it. He reached down, let his fingers fasten about the tube. With the greatest of care, he lifted it and began to catwalk back to the door of the vault.

But at the threshold Jimmy uttered a cry of alarm and swept Linda protectingly into his arms.

"What's the matter?" Garth demanded.

"The calibo-marset fire. Blue flame. It's started in the setro-frenalot. It's going to go off."

Garth's eyes shot wide with fear. He looked down at the tube in his hands, then abruptly swung and hurled it through the open doorway into the vault.

There was a low roar, mounting to a crescendo report. A cloud of smoke belched outward, and the ground beneath their feet trembled. At the first indication of Garth's action, Jimmy, Linda, and Hanley had hurled themselves backward, away from the vault door. Garth too had whirled and leaped like a released spring to safety.

But the two I.P. men were caught. They had not heard Jimmy's exclamation—hadn't time to guess what was coming. An avalanche of rubble and huge stones washed forward to sweep relentlessly over them. An instant later only a sound of dust-rising debris and masonry fragments marked the spot where they had stood.

As the deafening reverberations rolled back into silence, Hamilton Garth seemed to grasp the significance of the situation like a man in a dream. For a moment he stood there, rigid, eyes narrowing, lips quivering. Then with a snarl of profanity, he charged straight at Jimmy Starr.

Jimmy's head was still reeling dizzily from a blow dealt him by a flying chunk of rock, and he saw the onrushing Trust man through a haze. Garth's fist bludgeoned into his jaw. Another blow drove into his midsection, sent a wave of nausea sweeping through him. And then a picture of his father lying helpless on the study floor shot into his mind's eye; with it came a sudden realization of all that the *superiors* class—Garth's class—stood for. He snapped his fists forward and began to hit with all the strength he possessed at the face before him. He was still flailing his arms in and out, when Hanley stepped in and pulled him back.

*

It was the following morning, and the tracto-car was speeding smoothly down Canal Grand. In the driver's seat sat Jimmy Starr, a bandage on his temple, a smile on his face.

Beside him was Linda Hall, and in the rear tonneau Phil Hanley held a heat gun to cover the bound figure of Hamilton Garth.

"We did it," Jimmy said at length. "The figurine cache is destroyed forever."

The girl nodded.

"And the canal project won't be abandoned either," Jimmy continued. "That explosion opened up a shaft leading to a still lower crypt where there's enough pure *pxar* ingots stored to build all the canal locks the engineers need. Pure *pxar*. Not the figurine kind."

Linda nodded again.

"What I want to know is this," she said. "I know that that tube you threw into the vault didn't go off the first time because the detonator-cap didn't hit. But what kind of explosive is setro-frenalot? I never heard of it.

"Neither did I," Jimmy laughed. "It goes back to the juke box age of the twentieth century. In other words, double talk."